Text © 2002 by Diana Cohn.
Illustrations © 2002 by Amy Córdova.
Afterword copyright © 2002 by Shepard Barbash.
Photographs copyright © 1993 by Vicki Ragan.

The afterword is adapted from
Oaxacan Woodcarving: The Magic in the Trees
by Shepard Barbash, photography by Vicki Ragan,
published in 1993 by Chronicle Books.

Book design by Kristine Brogno.
Typeset in Zinjaro and Village Roman.
The illustrations in this book were rendered in
acrylic on a gessoed ground with color pencil.
Manufactured by Great Wall Printing, Hong Kong,
China, in December 2009.

Library of Congress Cataloging-in-Publication Data
Cohn, Diana.
Dream carver / by Diana Cohn ; illustrated by
Amy Córdova.
p. cm.
Summary: In this story, inspired by Oaxacan
wood carvers, a young boy dreams of colorful,
exotic animals that he will one day carve in wood.
ISBN 978-0-8118-1244-3
1. Jiménez, Manuel, 1919-   .-Juvenile fiction.
[1. Jiménez,Manuel, 1919-   .-Fiction. 2. Oaxaca de Juarez
(Mexico)—Fiction. 3.Mexico-Fiction. 4.Wood carving-Fiction.]
I. Córdova, Amy, ill. II. Title.
PZ7.C6649 Dr 2002
[E]—dc21
2001003884

10 9 8 7 6 5 4 3

This product conforms to CPSIA 2008.

Chronicle Books LLC
680 Second Street, San Francisco, California 94107

www.chroniclekids.com

To Ben, Annabel and Henry —D. C.

To Emma, Ben, Andrew and Sarah —A. C.

*For Manuel Jiménez, the visionary artist who inspired
a renaissance in Oaxacan wood carving; for Shepard
Barbash, Vicki Ragan and Jeanne Martinez for their
expertise and generosity; and for our photographer
and friend, Jennifer Beckman* —D. C. and A. C.

DREAM
CARVER

by Diana Cohn
illustrated by Amy Córdova

chronicle books · san francisco

"Whatever you can do, or dream you can, begin it.
Boldness has genius, power and magic in it.
Begin it now." —Goethe

ateo lived in a small village in Mexico nestled beneath
the ancient Zapotec city of Monte Alban. His family grew
blue corn and green alfalfa in the fields outside their *casa*.

Every sunrise, when the rackety rooster crowed, Mateo joined his father to carve little toys, *juguetes,* which they sold at village *fiestas* and to the tourists who came from all over the world to see the great Zapotec ruins.

Like many of the wood-carvers in their village, Mateo and his father carved tiny pigs, cats, dogs and goats—carvings so small they could fit in the palm of a hand. Mateo's sister and mother, like many of the women in their village, painted the carvings in bright, bold colors.

Mateo loved the village *fiestas* because those were the only times when there were so many delicious things to eat. He feasted on turkey with black *mole* sauce and drank hot chocolate until his belly ached.

He danced to the village band and laughed as his mother and father put their fingers in their ears when PUM! PUM! PUM! the fireworks and bottle rockets exploded one after the other in the *zocalo*, the village square.

In the days between the *fiestas*, Mateo learned as much as he could about all the animals he saw around his village. He watched how his herd of goats stretched their necks to drink water and how jackrabbits

darted this way and that across the fields. He saw how cats rolled in the dusty grass and how dogs lay down to rest lazily in the shade.

Whenever Mateo sat under his favorite *guaje* tree, a parade of these animals pranced through his imagination. The goats were as pink as bougainvillea with cactus-green speckles, the jackrabbits were cloaked

in orange capes with red-and-white flames, and the cats were as purple as eggplants with spots of corn yellow. "Someday," Mateo promised himself, "I will carve all these animals to life!"

One morning, Mateo told his father about his dreams. "Papa," he said, "I see animals so big and so bright that I will need to carve them with a *machete!* I want to make them my way, instead of making the same *juguetes* we carve over and over."

Mateo's father said, "Why should you carve differently when for hundreds of years it has worked for us to carve the way I taught you? We work in the fields all day and barely have enough time to make *juguetes* for the *fiestas* and for Señora Martinez to sell in her shop in Oaxaca. So stop these foolish dreams. We have work to do!"

But Mateo couldn't stop the animals from creeping and crawling through his dreams. They visited him everywhere, in the fields during the day and in his dreams as he fell asleep at night. One night, a dazzling gold-and-rose-colored jaguar called out to Mateo,

"Carve me **grand and wild,** and you will find the power and strength you need to **carve all your dreams.**"

So the next morning, Mateo joined his father and carved miniature *juguetes* as he had always done. But in the afternoon, he snuck away and cut a giant branch of fresh green wood from the *copalillo* tree and peeled it with his *machete*. With a few bold *machetazos*, he tried to carve the mighty jaguar that had been in his dreams the night before,

but it looked clumsy. Next he tried to carve an armadillo, but it looked lifeless. Then he tried to carve a chicken, but it looked crooked. "Why don't you come out the way I want you to?" he cried, as he threw his half-carved animals to the ground.

But Mateo kept carving day after day and week after week, until finally, one day, as he carved the *quetzal*, the iridescent bird of the rain forest, the wood peeled off like feathers. Mateo sanded the bird smooth and then took out his paintbrush.

He painted the bird turquoise and orange with yellow dots sprinkled across her breast. He painted her long feathers in bright-green-and-black stripes. Mateo could hardly believe his eyes. At last, he had carved an animal from his dreams to life!

Now the carving came easier. When Mateo imagined a
white-polka-dotted squirrel or an orange-striped gazelle

gazing at the stars or a black and yellow-spotted frog bracing to spring, he could carve them all just like that!

But what Mateo loved best of all was when he had no idea what to carve. He would sit and look at his woodpile until he sensed an animal waiting there for him.

Then Mateo would start to carve … and carve … and carve some more, until he said, "*Hola conejito!*" and a little rabbit would pop right out of the wood as if waking from a deep sleep.

One day, Mateo looked at his animals and wondered what his father would think of them. Would he be surprised? Would he be angry?

The next *fiesta* was *Día de los Muertos*, Day of the Dead, the perfect chance to display his carvings.

Mateo could barely sleep the night before the festival, but in the early dawn, just before the rooster crowed, Mateo finally fell into a light sleep. Very softly, he heard a raven call out to him,

"You have **nothing to fear**. Your *dream animals* are with you."

That morning, Mateo gathered his carvings and laid them down on the main street for all to see. As the *fiesta* began, musicians gathered together and people flocked through the *zocalo*. When the children saw Mateo's carvings, their eyes lit up. Like honeybees attracted to

sticky, sweet *fiesta* candy, they swarmed to see the animals and began to name them and to play with them as if they were alive. Wood-carvers marveled at the magical creatures. The noisy, chattering crowd surrounded Mateo and bought one carving after another.

Finally, when all the bustle and clamor began to calm, Mateo felt a gentle hand on his shoulder. When he turned around, he saw his father's beaming face. "Mateo," his father said, "it's time for you to teach me a new way to carve!"

"Papa," Mateo said, remembering the early mornings when his father first taught him to carve, "I saved my favorite carving of all for you."

And Mateo picked up the *quetzal* and placed it in his father's hands.

OAXACAN WOOD CARVING
THE MAGIC IN THE TREES

Shepard Barbash

Dry and mountainous Oaxaca (pronounced wa-HAH-ka) is one of Mexico's largest and poorest states, yet its folk-art tradition is among the richest. Stretching out from the capital city, which is also called Oaxaca, the Oaxacan valley nurtures an astonishing diversity of crafts: pottery, fireworks, jewelry, cloth, baskets, candles—and wood carving.

Oaxacans have carved children's toys and religious masks for hundreds, perhaps thousands, of years. The style that dominates today, however, can be traced back to a single man, Manuel Jiménez.

It was Jiménez who first used the wood that all the carvers now use, *copalillo*. It was Jiménez who moved beyond the popular tradition of miniature toy making. And it was Jiménez who established the international market for all the carvers who came after him.

Manuel Jiménez

It wasn't easy. For thirty-five years, Jiménez was among the poorest peasants in a very poor village. As a boy, Jiménez herded goats and made models of his flock in clay. As a young man, he would go barefoot into the hills to forage for weeds and grasshoppers.

Even in a successful carver's family, no one is idle: father and sons carve; mother and daughters paint; smaller children and elders

An original carving by Manuel Jiménez

sand. And they have their farmwork. Remarkably, the carving boom has not done much to upset the region's farming tradition. Most carvers, no matter how successful, continue to grow their own food and herd their own animals as their fathers and grandfathers did before them.

"Carving is in a peasant's blood," says Alejandrino Fuentes, an engineer who left his profession to carve. "A peasant carries his machete like a friend, as a student would carry a pen or a book. You sit there watching the animals eat grass. Sometimes you're in the shade of a tree, and maybe you see a branch that looks like an animal—let's say a monkey. Purely by instinct you cut it down and start to whittle. You do it to pass the time, so that you're not out there falling asleep. But that's where the inspiration begins, that's where wood carving is born."

María Jiménez (no relation to Manuel) is famous for the wild and colorful patterns she paints on her brothers' carvings. Like so many others, María started out copying her neighbors by covering her figures with polka dots. They sold poorly. "But then," she recalls, "one morning we went out in the fields. It was a beautiful day...barely raining. The desert looks wonderful in the rain. There were flowers, green leaves, yellow stalks, so many colors. And I asked myself, 'How can I do it like this? How can I paint like this?' That's how I started. That's how we all start, probably—by seeing the beauty around us."